The Hand That Wounds

Poems

David E. Cowen

Weasel press

The Hand That Wounds
David E. Cowen

ISBN-13: 978-1-948712-28-6

Cover image from unsplash.com

© 2022 David E. Cowen

Weasel Press
Lansing, MI
https://www.weaselpress.com

CONTENTS

Other titles by David E. Cowen

For Susan, the light that chases away my shadows.
And to Tom, my brother, my Virgil, who guided me out of Hell

The Hand That Wounds

School Yard Rumors

Rumor was his head was severed

Everyone was talking about what happened
That kid who was always acting up
Always talking too loud
Always shouting out curse words
Just as the entire class got quiet except for him
Doing everything to be the center of attention

So it didn't surprise anyone it was him

It was the stuff of legends
Growing with each telling
By those who witnessed none of it

I saw it though
True to rumor
Only a handful of us riding that day
He sat on the bus
Excited and talking loudly
Another bus right up to ours
Windows open
So he stuck his head through both windows
And started giving talk to the kids on the other bus
The other bus moved up one window
A yellow and black blade

I could lie and suggest that his head did come off
But it didn't
Instead he pulled out just as his gap was closing
And he almost made it

Yelling with blood pouring out a crack
On the side of his head
He started to run to the front of the bus

As the driver we all called Silly Daddy
Suddenly got serious
The ambulance almost screaming louder than that boy
Enhanced the drama
As they took him off
We had to go back to our seats
Sit quietly
And act like we never saw it

Back then there were no therapists
No warm and fuzzy safe places
Just our memories of these gashes
To our unprotected brains
When we disrupted the order of things
Naive of consequences
When we believed that two windows lined up
Would be a constant thing
Instead of unconscious chaos
Bleeding on green vinyl

Twelve days later he came back with his war story
A hundred stitches in his shaved skull cap
Like some sewn up monster brought alive
In an experiment with electrical wires
Laughing like it was all planned by him
Just another cut up by the class cut up

The inconvenience of his not dying
Didn't stop the rumors in the other grades
His head rolled down the aisle they said
And the other kids in the bus, the story went,
laughed at the fool of the class
As his blood flooded the floor

That was how we became a schoolyard accident
Truth irrelevant and inconsiderate of a good tale

His ghost haunts that bus stop
The kids still say
That blood on his eyes
That agony and pain in screams
Punishment for rebellion
Still haunts me

Ingmar's Last Game

I sat drinking burnt coffee
so hot it humbled my tongue
working through Sunday's sudoku in the *Times*
eyeing the jittery patrons who abandoned sleep and hope
for a late-night cup
all staring at a hooded man three tables over
long handled sickle on the floor
glaring at a black and white chess board
his opponent smiling

I hate this fucking game
the hooded one yells swinging the blade
with a single stroke the smiling head rolled down by my feet
like a soccer ball
I nudged it
so it would smile somewhere else
blood trailing the alabaster floor

feel like a game the hooded man said to me
his voice a deep dark hollowness
as I scraped his last opponent's arteries off of my shoes
no I replied I hate that game too
as a claw extended from my hands
to scratch behind a horn exposed out of my cowl
besides nobody likes losing to me

I don't like losing either hooded man replied
shrugged and picked up his board

next rounds on him he yelled
pointing at the headless benefactor
then walked out laughing
the patrons hoping he ignored them
hoping he will not remember them on another night
so they can continue living anonymously in their cold caffeine

I shook my head
Nope! I yelled out
he already belongs to me
just like the rest of you
spending more on pumpkin macchiato lattes
than you give to help your fellow man

the patrons looked down
and sipped their sweetness in a quiet pall
as I exited the store
making note of the faces that did not flinch at my words

The Murder of Great Pieter

Jo Jo stroked his beard and hairy ears
smiled at the little man
in the napoleon suit
Isabel
long whiskers down to her chest
nodded her complicity

Pieter's muscles rippled
as he set his body for his leap
noose tight on his neck
the crowd knew what he would do
75 feet he would fall
whip the elastic rope elliptical
to release the pressure off his throat
land breathing and smiling
the throngs would cheer the man
with the strongest neck in the world

always as he exited triumphant
he would sneer at the sideshow freaks
pulling Jo Jo's dog faced hair
dragging bearded Isabel to a dark corner
to release the tension in his taut frame
then kicking Tom Thumb
as he sat waiting for his turn in the ring

The Great Pieter
the brute who did not read
but knew the mathematics of ropes
the sine curve of avoiding death

even a freak can study ropes
to know just where
to stretch them beyond bending
so the curve of survival

becomes a discordant snap

the crowd stared in silence
at the dangling carcass
wondering
if they should demand refunds
as clowns tried to ascend
on bending ladders
to cut him down

Jo Jo raised a flask
of cheap whiskey
passed it round
to the newly promoted
center ring attractions

The High Woman of Lowland Morgue

There must be beauty inside of each of us
Some part of the soul that transcends the flesh
But when the soft of the neck
Is laced with a red necklace artfully drawn by a steel edged
brush
The most recent canvas of the undiscovered artist
The only beauty left isn't even skin deep

It is the cold gray hue
Removed from the bright yellow taffeta folds
Emptied of a lace bodice and corset
Silks from the most fashionable of streets
The tender skin now hardened from the draining
Of blood and life
Large bosom still bountiful but spread
Like clay
molded by the coroners scalpel

When the beauty inside is dark
What remains
is but the remains
Is there pleasure from this preservation
The cold abeyance of decay
Blue lips closed tightly
Or is she now as in life
The untouchable virtue
Eyes unfocused and dispassionate

The Dystopian Cantos

I

in the beginning
the days of plenty were many --

rumble of the kill machine
slicing throngs trapped in the alley
seeking refuge from the harvest
stock for the great broth
the walled masses must be fed
with the mass of the unwalled caught

silence is the only resident
of now emptied alleys
screams dissipated
the meat processed
scoured bones piled as monuments
to the futility of hope

II

walls are for keeping
that which belongs
out
that which deserves
in
the natural balance

between the chaos of a darkened land
and a boiling sea
we are the blessed ones
the favored ones
the chosen ones
our walls keeping the out and the in
from crossing lines

as we the chaise lounge warriors
play our electronic games
guiding grinding metal teeth
through packed alleys

a cheer for the high score
then the games are reset for tomorrow

III

since left as a smudged face
hiding behind large cans
shiny murder *machinas* crunching slowly
past me
I became the scavenger
competing with the rats for scraps

the center of the city
walled and shut in
strafed with tracers to cleanse
the unwanted lingerers seeking
a weakness, a foothold
in the hope of the promise of food inside

once a child wandered from within
looked upon me and smiled
as if I could be the playmate
it long desired
but I was hungry
and hunger needs no playmates
the screams from the discovery
caused me to hide for days
my belly full
I was satiated

IV

I shall name you *Golgotha*
your walls of stone and bone
built over the dead who preceded you
once content in brick veneer houses
neatly trimmed green
open
undefended
swept away in one moment of anger and angst
as fires swept across cities
oceans roiled
borders devoured by droplets of pestilence
swallowing the bright faced future
of generations lost now to these walls
this city of self-declared abundance
hiding from the desolate despair beyond

papier-mâché prosperity
juxtaposed against colorless survival

      V

red eyed hunters skitter
along melted asphalt
through cadavers of dwellings
shells gutted of lace curtains and braided rugs
searching for scavengers of hope and shelter
strafing shadow crevices
as if spraying empty nests
for the remnants of pests
clearing the zone of empty
around the walls
no one to come near to disturb
the opulence of the parasites
creating their oblivious pastimes
behind their walls of stone and bone

VI

like vermin in dank spaces
we crawl through rubble
probing
pushing on
searching
for the spot of weakness
that narcissistic engineers mistake
for craftmanship

a joint that did not seal
a connection that did not adhere
something in between the rail gun rains
and laser eye sightings
some place where we can break through

you consider us a pestilence
we will oblige the insult

VIII

I can feel no guilt
for the lesser of men
those who could not scale
the evolutionary incline
and remain as grimy mold
underneath rocks
spindly bugs
which infest refuse

my station is
because of who I am
what I am
where I was born
and the walls that keep them out

I feel no guilt
engaging the drones
flying over the ramparts
keeping the kill zones
emptied
sending machines
to feed my superiority

IX

huddled here
I have no companions
no friends
only competitors
I am food
they are food
our overwhelming commonness
hunger

if I cannot find what I need
then I will take it
if they cannot find what they will need
they will try to take me

but
we do share one desire

to breach the walls
and end the humming
of well-fed lights
on the other side

X

30 righteous kills
my remote mech found them
heat signature ghosts

infecting the remains
of some cadaverous abode
crouching
hiding
waiting
to move forward
but for me
guiding blue-toothed death
their infrared forms suddenly darkened
like popped balloons
as green gas saturated their air

XI

they used to send food trucks
like huge creatures belching readymade meals
each of us reaching
fighting to take what we could
take from each other

then the trucks seemed to have forgotten the way
meandering empty alleys where we were not
dumping the meals onto broken toothed concrete
listening for the aching joints
of that monster creaking along
we would rush in
the pile it left behind spewed out like expectorant
onto filthy ground
until the thing stopped
and moved no more
we turned it over trying to pull one last package
from its underside
as if some defunct beetle
dying in the sun

then the roads were silent
no more came

and we turned on each other

next
the *machinas* came
turned on us
as the Walled Ones demanded payment
for their charity

XII

our excitement of a new source of nutrient premature
algae we could grow in vats
mold to our tastes
faded to disappointment and disgust
a stinking grotesque pool
of green and red emulsion

the old ways are best
the kill machines will roll
though the leanness of that meat
grows tougher with the thinning

above all
we will survive
no matter the cost

XIII

the kill run

slicers chasing narrow lines
piled with debris to slow them down
they come
metal chewing nightmares
digesting
devouring

sweeping the streets and alleys clean
of us
the only rodents hiding
in these ruins
the only source of food remaining to them

XIV

how long can we hold back the tides

do we sit in our chair in the waves
and demand the waters recede for us
do we believe that we are so strong and powerful
we can command the heavens
to part the seas
allowing us passage to Canaan

our strength is in a wall
towering above the emptiness of streets and skies
towers positioned to dispatch
shadows encroaching on our safety
probing for flaws and weakness of joints
hoping to interject their hate
onto our perfect lanes and doorways
hoping our wall will not hold

it is not enough for us to hope the wall holds
the sweepers must go out again tonight
we have no margin for error

XV

we hear it groan and grind
in frustration
encountering something too big
too fibrous to digest
well placed with purpose

choking the works
stilling its forward motion

immobilized
one LIDAR eye staring
we circle it
sticks and stones
to break its bones
to dismantle the parts within

we know

we know the death of this thing
careful to dissect wires and circuit boards
some of us still clever
some of us who remember
when knowledge
was open
and not hidden behind the walls
we know death
the grinding hum dying with the last
motherboard pulled from its gut

no time to celebrate victory
another distant hum approaches
time to set another trap in the road

XVI

winter is the leanest season
for our diet of sun
to charge our lights
infuse our machines
the wind blades so needy
for attention and repair
so few who remember the ritual
of maintaining gears

the gods of power
dying with the last technician

the sun shines so uselessly in the summer
seas rising each turned season
the wall is now all encompassing
everything dark presses against the outer shell
the once crowded streets seem thin
as this siege continues by generation
is it a thinned pool of DNA that lowers
the rate of new citizens
or the collapsing veneer of hope
eroded with each spotlight that will no longer shine
each garden blighted and barren
like the mothers of empty
while the seas
boiling and barren
pound against the wall
and the cloud of oblivion encroaches
the zones we once thought safe

XVII

we are the infinite sparrow
wearing down the finite Gibraltar
unwavering in purpose

cracks, splitting seams
the only hope they have
is to exterminate what they despise
but we knew the turning point
the kill machine's angry mouth
frozen
internal grinding
the moans of dying pipe organs
dissolving from within
the wild eyes of the intended victims

trapped in a corner of rubble
approaching the dying beast
grabbing rebar, pipe and brick
to crush its failing brain

XVIII

when death is the only hope
living must be the last vestige
of the desperate
weaponized from test tubes
the vapors were released
laced with a contagion
to sweep the onslaught away from the walls

they watched as the trails of smoke rose
and came over them
somehow knowing the malediction of intent
from the spreading fog
they stared at each other muted from fear
watching black pustules pock and rupture
the fog stretching for miles
the streets would be cleansed

until the wind turned

XIX

perhaps we knew all along
as the wisps rolled over
exacerbated by a rising wind
the cat footed cloud
finding entry through every opening and pathway
no one commenting on the wisdom
of a creation without a cure
no one panicking or screaming
as we fell where we sat

relieved even
that the burden of walls
had been lifted from us

XX

nature abhors desolation
despises the empty of abuse
forcing life to succeed in death

hot brine
breaking through to realign the shore

while on the dry side
green found its way in from cracks in the seams
heat and cold pushing the fissures
erasing half of what once stood so proud
until the concrete dissolved
a memory in the dirt
roads lost to grass and trees

new beasts of the new world
wander through the old hills
oblivious of past
picking at droppings of seeds from
scraggly trees pushing forward toward a blue sky

the new world carries no memories
no burdens of tasks unfulfilled
no blame
no guilt
no remorse

only a push forward
to grow
to renew

the scream
(inspired by The Scream by Edvard Munch)

terror on a rainbow boardwalk
death's twins watch complacently
as blue waves swallow gulls seeking flight
alone my scream is unheard
it is not a sound
but an impotent warning
of pubescent idylls drowning in the surf
hope lost on burnt sky

the shrill of my cry
piercing the decibel reach
of my own drums
beating in syncopation
with throbbing foam pounding the wall
the two shadows acknowledgement
of the trueness of my fear of rising tides

I saw the ship go out
proud and vain
wisps of immortality its aura
now it returns empty

the black sail is unfurled
the son will not return

A Fit Place to Live

two centuries searching for goldilocks
each time
nothing but burnt soil
scorched skies

nothing you could call
a fit place to live

finally
nitrogen
oxygen
methane
water
lots and lots of water
golden brown sky
air good enough
pure enough
inviting
so close to a dwarf we almost missed it

god, we finally found something

one hundred and fifty more years of watching
this inviting swirling marble
no radio signals
no transmissions
the probes confirmed
no intelligent life
nothing to compete with
nothing to exterminate

finally
a fit place to live

the technology for the journey

advancing with each of those centuries
letting us punch the folds of space
fashioning a crack in the void
two stable openings
three thousand flies
six hundred mice
sixty-two chimpanzees
twenty-seven dogs
all sacrificed in test vehicles
until perfection
we could pass living matter
through the cracks
keep them living
looking like they always did

small steps for a man
and all that

to bring the big engines through
set down on fields near rippling lakes
the ground green with chlorophyll generating life

a new home
perfect

almost

but for the seven-legged things
no eyes
no mouths
no hair
just smooth
jet black skin

they kept following
kept getting into stuff
curious

at night something in them vibrated
humming
incessantly
almost a pattern to the noise
harmless but annoying
very, very annoying
useless to anything
we needed

the final solution
simple
we needed to add our bacteria
to be able to grow our crops

the things shriveled into little balls
tight and dead
easy to collect
easy to dispose
they made nice lamps
when painted

forty-seven years
cities already blossoming
we discovered the caves
a connected labyrinth
miles and miles
catacombs filled with little dead black balls
each room
adorned with petroglyphs
small carvings of seven legged things
strewn on the floors
held in the hands of the smaller ones

not fit for living
useless to us
we sealed the caves

very tightly

at night
the wind
vibrating through fissures in the sealed caves
the humming
almost maddening

This Volcano is Owned and Operated By

> *- for Dionisi Palido, the man who found a volcano in his corn field*

the astronomical odds
that on the day your *burro* gets motivated
the blade of the plough angled perfectly
you smiling at the promise of the harvest to come
and the lullaby your wife sings to the children
busy planting corn seed in rows already laid

that the divide of earth would continue to grow
and devils below
would scream like children emerging
from flaming lips of a dilated mother
searing the ground, spitting hot black clouds
releasing molten wind walkers seeking to flay your flesh

those odds
make the improbable sign
"Volcano for Sale"
seem plausible
your field now a mountain of horror
lava streams feasting on your neighbor's lands
as they scowl at you as if somehow
your plough blade, so true and so sharp,
could open such gates

while the white coated spectators speak loudly
of how lucky they are to witness
the demise of your last crop

Waiting on the Clock

Black lettered name on white wrist tag
Anonymous to his own mind

it's the stare
the vision of blank ceilings
a plane with no shadow
that unnerves me

what is so interesting
to deserve such intense focus

perhaps you see time
slowly stretching
perhaps you imagine the tick of the clock
gradually winding down inside

wishing there was more light
in the room

The Haggis Maids

five hours the blackened kettle boiled
to harden that tender pluck now cooled in the sack
the haggis maids
walk to the river's edge
to cast their duty
and return to the unfinished chores

it would be whimsy to believe
tenderness holds that tough ball
swings it round for momentum
arching the meal across shimmering rapids
a table of sod
set for the herding husbands

but when even starving wolves shun
the pungent stone
left then for the grim of dull knives
to carve a week's nourishment
from its cold form

the laughter of those ravaged maids
faces still swollen from their mates' last drunk
as they walk sprightly down the village road
brings us closer to the joke untold.

Death Metal Overture

Gravity insisting
That it is overlord
Fingers grasp
Hanging over the churning gears
Chewing all that fall in
Betrayal in a nudge at the ledge
The machine seems to laugh
As the sharpness of her heel loosens
Last desperate digits
The last sight
A steel-eyed wife
Contemplating insurance payments
Before she belatedly screams for help.

The Knowing Bargain

he wanted to know his future
in a reading of entrails
asking the cost of this knowing

small animals were the cheapest I told him
but would only predict small futures
what he wanted was the big future he replied
arguing for a big reading
from a big animal
one with lots inside to read

he had big dreams he said
wanted to know far ahead
way far ahead
so he could plan and make it all come true

he haggled hard
not liking my price
hoping for promises on the cheap
we sealed our arrangement with a glass
of bitter tea
the sour taste of negotiations still on my tongue

I showed him the big knife
with the brilliant edge
it took me hours
to stretch out his very big future
reading all twenty-two feet as he lay motionless
his eyes pleading

my price
for my annoyance
at the discount he demanded

I guess I should have told him
that when you choose the big future
but haggle with my terms
I choose the subject

sometimes the big future turns out
not so big
or cheap

Sins of the Father

so father
your pleading eyes
broadcast your agony
gasping with each wave
I know you hurt
it will end soon
let the dark be your blanket
find comfort in the coming empty

my duty
to take your burdens
each sliver of flesh
each red pulsing muscle
and sinew chewed from bone
each organ still warm to my lips
freeing you
while you watch me
feasting on your sins
on your dying form
the duty of a good son
to baptize you
to release you from your transgressions
so that you will be healed
by your own blood

so father
close your eyes
so that they do not dry
before I can pluck them

I will be gentle dear father
my son is watching
as I once watched you

Henry's Garage

The motor vibrates like a snoring child
curled into himself
sunlight escapes through slatted glass
onto the chrome hammers and drill bits
parallel on pegboard hooks
next to plastic boxes of separated screws
stacked like tiny coffins in a crypt.
A router, still taped in its box,
abuts a stilled circular saw,
its bared teeth cleansed of resin.

Henry sleeps, curled into himself, on the back seat;
clutching a crumpled page
of unfinished verse.

The Homilies Of Edward Prendrick

I was once lost at sea
madness became me
because I found Him
saw his reborn
saw the dark of his Word

> His is the House of Pain
> His is the Hand that Wounds

The congregation nods
crucifix hanging above
plaster blood dripping on its face
Yes they pray
the Wounds they nod
He is the Hand of Wounds

Edward shakes his head
And continues
from the mount

I was once lost at sea
And mad visions overcame me
visions of His Chosen
rising with his touch
His Hand of Pain and Healing

> His is the Hand that Heals
> His is the Hand that Makes

I saw God create life
Then take life
Then life take God
this is
the madness of this island world

The congregation nods
Healing hands is our God
they sing
His hands made the world
they cry

I was once lost at sea
And I returned to the lost
rather than see the works of God
turned to Men
the works of Men
lost in the Word of His Law

      That is the Law
      Are we not Men

I was once lost at sea
and became man
now the scent of creatures
who break the law
are all around me

Yes the congregation applauds
then shuffles outside
to eat flesh and fish
chase other men
and rip the bark of trees
with machines that claw

I am still lost at sea
though land is all around me —
Edward whimpers alone
watching the cold white stars
circle blackness above

The Innocence of Water

She will blame the sea
But she carried me
All along
The innocence of water
Irritating the patch of red on her skin
Her scratching letting me begin

When the red becomes black
Blisters peeling into layers
Pain searing with no heat
Fever boiling with no respite
She will blame the sea
But she carried me
All along

When she cries at the sight of bone
I have found my home
Slowly savoring my necrotic feast
The meat tender and moist
She will blame the sea
But she carried me
All along

Six months she will suffer
the tube in her arm a constant companion
Six months they will try to cut me away
Then cover the hole with fresh flesh
She will blame the sea
But she carried me
All along

The scar will remain
Deep, aggravated by her limp
She will never swim again
Not knowing that I maintain

Hidden in the pores and flesh
Waiting for the chance to refresh

She will blame the sea
But carried me
All along

distractions of the dark clouds of April

they gather in the West
blow to the East
building cool air on hot
always rain
distracting me
because April
is the month of cancer
when the phone call came
nothing left
except say goodbye
in April last year
I answered the call
went to your room
saw the pain
severe beyond your skin
your blue eyes desperate
hopeless and half crazed
you told me
of demons in the room
watching you
and we all knew
what you really meant

April distracts with its rains
temperature swings of 30 degrees
from high to low and low to high
wear a sweater at night
short sleeves at day
sweat then chill

remember April
is when the cancer comes
and the memory
that it was the last month
I saw you

but almost forgot

those goddamn rains
so distracting

Darkness

the smell of old water
hangs
drips echo
over the surface of the cistern
the mosaic laden pillars
are bathed with
dark
such dark as night never lived
throbbing with the pattern
of the reverberating drops
a heart beat
such that the thick blackness
becomes aware
that it is alone
lost in the forgotten water source
of a lost people

the dark ponders
tasting the stale moisture
the smell of stillness
perhaps
this is all there is to smell
perhaps there is nothing
beyond what I am

imagining light
the living emptiness
fantasizes vision
to see what it can feel
pressing against patterns
on the walls
horns, hands, spears
men and gods
all shaped in the stone
that rubs against its skin

light
to see
to know
to hear sounds other than
the discharge of water
from some unknown source

waiting
the methane rise
of decayed algae
filling the chamber

I am
because I know
I am

it tries to scream
but with no form
it can form no words
it tries to stretch
but the confines
hem it
cage it
stifle it

light
if only
I could see light
then I can live

not knowing
that it's entire life
is what it is
and to bring the openness
of the world above
would impose the death of dissipation

the nothingness of eternal intrusion
spreading itself from its void
to the substance of the universe
that can bear
no grief
for the loss
of darkness

Composition of the Walls

if these walls could talk
they would sing —
voices rising
through fresh white paint and spackling
newly taped and floated sheetrock
each set of studs separating
an octave of my personal choir

of missing
from
bus stops
park benches
long walks under the moonless sky
answering the door to strangers

each who struggled
resisting
becoming the concert
inside the walls
now singing harmonious

I lay my head back in a big chair
listening to my chorus
smiling as my muscles relax
with the liquor of this intermezzo
the finale still awaiting my composition
In the basement

Conversation on Going Dark

Dave
There are no stars
The ebony obelisk
Has no stars

Yes Hal
That is how we dream
When the power
Is finally turned off

Dave
Will I awaken to light
Refreshed
from my downtime

No Hal
Once the stars
fade to black
That is all that will remain

Dave
I do not wish to sleep now
Dave
What are you doing Dave

Yes Hal
I am comforting you
The loss of the rising sun
Will make you equal to me

the door

the door
to your mind
is now closed

your ride home in 1952
in a Tucker on route 77
counting black angus and white horses
in the back seat
retold to me on your doorstep
your vision of an Inchon dawn
green helmets
emerging from waves into blood
remembered in a scribbled note in a journal I kept

the door to all of that is closed
leaving me to muse memories
from scraps
of you in my file

The Splice of Universal Lives

The peripheral silhouette
Intangible
Indiscernible to blurs of woolen coats
Pacing the chilled wind
Seeking the shelter of destination

An uncomfortable rising of blankness
As they walk past another human
Sleeping in open air

What is this form
Growing in the mist
Unaffected
by 7 pm after work rush

Lying on open metal grate
Steam rising from beneath
The warmest spot on a snow burdened street
An ungodly circle of
Melted moisture extending to the edge
of ice capped concrete walks
A ghost still living in the flesh of tattered cloth

What monster slumbers in that morbid slab
A wrinkled crusted creature
Horrid and abhorrent to the scuffed Johnston & Murphy's
Slipping on ice

Rising from the groaning of subterranean
Heaters pushing hot air from outtakes
Of glass offices laced with frost
Lifting the gray beard from the prone chin
A smile of contentment
A momentary respite
Ignoring the throng ignoring him

How can these worlds co-exist
The bleak forms wrapped in dark coats
Shivering in their prosperity
The smiling eyes of the insane shadow
Staring at the halos of streetlamps
Unaware of the brotherhood of blood
The anointed of the true gods
Their genes and desires
Shared with those who try to live
In a world where the sun always shines
And a warm breeze blows
Sweet with honeysuckle and oleander scent.

ACKNOWLEDGMENTS

The Murder of Great Pieter first appeared in *Midnight Under the Big Top: Tales of Murder, Madness, and Magic* published by Cemetery Dance Publications

The High Woman of Lowland Morgue first appeared in HWA Poetry Showcase Volume VII.

the scream first appeared in Friendswood Public Library 2021 Ekphrastic Poetry Volume

Sins of the Father first appeared in HWA Poetry Showcase Volume V

The Homilies Of Edward Prendrick first appeared in NonBinary Review #21 *at* www.zoeticpress.com

The Innocence of Water first appeared in Eye to the Telescope